The Pet-Sitting Service

PET-SITTING SERVICE

Text copyright © 1996 by Danae Dobson

Illustrations copyright © by Karen Loccisano

Library of Congress Cataloging-in-Publication Data

Dobson, Danae.
   The pet-sitting service / Danae Dobson ; illustrated by Karen Loccisano.
     p. cm. — (The Sunny Street Kids' Club ; 2)
"Word kids!"
Summary: The Sunny Street Kids' Club needs to earn some money, but when
Conner comes up with a plan to start a pet-sitting business in his house without
asking his parents, big problems follow.
   ISBN 0–8499–5113–5
   [1. Pet Sitting—Fiction. 2. Parent and child—Fiction 3. Christian life—Fiction.]
I. Loccisano, Karen, ill.   II. Title.   III. Series: Dobson, Danae.   Sunny Street Kids'
Club ; 2.
PZ7.D6614Pe   1996
[Fic]—dc20   95–37634
                                           CIP
                                           AC

Printed in Hong Kong

96 97 98 99 00 PLP 9 8 7 6 5 4 3 2 1

The Pet-Sitting Service

by
Danae Dobson

Illustrated by Karen Loccisano

WORD PUBLISHING
Dallas·London·Vancouver·Melbourne

The Sunny Street Kids' Club was facing
a big problem. They had lots of wonderful things
they wanted to do—but no money.

Connor Riley, the president of the club, called a
special meeting to order. Included in the club were
Connor; his little brother, Ryan; Stephanie; Matthew;
and Lauren. Then, there was Rusty, the Rileys' golden
retriever. He served as the mascot.

Connor began the meeting. "Our club planned to go to the zoo this week," he said, "But we only have one dollar and fifty-eight cents. We need to come up with a plan to raise money quick!" Connor said.

"Why don't we do a lemonade stand?" suggested Lauren.

"No, everybody does that," said Matthew.

"Well, my sister makes a lot of money baby-sitting," said Stephanie.

"That's it! A sitting service," said Connor.

"I can't baby-sit. I'm only six," whined Ryan.

"No, silly," said Connor. "Let's pet-sit."

"Oh boy!" said Ryan. "We'll have a zoo right here!" Connor frowned at his brother.

"Okay, here's how it will work," said Connor. "When people go on trips, they'll call us to take care of their animals. We'll charge them, and—"

"Where will the animals stay?" interrupted Stephanie.

"Right here in our basement," answered Connor.

"But what will your parents say?" asked Matthew.

"They won't care," said Connor. "I don't even need to ask."

The rest of the afternoon was spent making flyers and posting them around the neighborhood. Even Rusty was helping.

By the end of the day, each family had received an ad for the pet-sitting service.

PET SITTING

PET SITTING

Connor yawned as he sat down in the front yard
with his friends.

"Well," he said. "We're all finished. Now we just
have to wait for the phone calls."

"What if someone wants us to keep alligators or
snakes?" Matthew asked.

"Don't be silly," replied Connor. "There are no
alligators in this part of town, and I'm not afraid of
snakes."

That evening at supper, Mr. Riley asked Connor and Ryan about their day.

"Well," said Connor, clearing his throat. "Today we had a club meeting, and . . ."

Ryan couldn't wait any longer. He blurted out the news about the pet-sitting service.

"What?" said Mr. Riley. "Connor, you didn't ask your mother and me if you could bring animals in the house. Why didn't you check with us first?"

"I thought it would be okay," answered Connor.

"Well, I'm afraid it's *not* okay," said Mrs. Riley. "This is a home, not a kennel."

"Please, Mom?" begged Connor. "The animals will stay in the basement, and we'll do *all* the work. We'll take them for walks and make sure they have food and everything. . . ."

Mr. and Mrs. Riley looked at each other.

"Can we try it for just one week?" asked Ryan. "*Please?*"

Mr. Riley was quiet for a moment. Finally he took a deep breath.

"Well, all right," he said. "One week!"

"And don't forget what you promised," added Mrs. Riley.

Connor and Ryan were so excited, they barely heard their parents. They could hardly wait for the weekend to arrive!

By Friday afternoon, the Sunny Street Kids' Club had received several phone calls. They would have animals to pet-sit for the weekend!

Connor and his friends worked hard to get ready for their jobs. They cleaned the basement, swept the floor, and set up sleeping areas for animals.

At four o'clock, the doorbell
rang. Everyone followed Connor as
he ran up the stairs. By the time they
got to the door, Mrs. Riley had already
answered it.

"Why, hello, Mrs. Bloomfield," she said.

In walked a very stuffy-looking woman
holding a large, white cat.

"I'm here to drop off Tootsie," said Mrs. Bloomfield. "Is this where the pet service is?"

"Yes, ma'am," answered Connor.

Mrs. Bloomfield wasted no time in giving dozens of instructions about her precious Tootsie. She even wanted the children to give the cat a bath!

Finally, she left and everyone was glad to see her go.

In a few minutes, the doorbell rang again. This time it was Mr. Curtis. He had two pets with him—a parrot named Pierre and a bloodhound named Sarge.

Connor promised to take good care of them as Mr. Curtis waved good-bye.

The children took the animals to the basement. But right away, everything started to go wrong!

Sarge didn't like Rusty, and neither one of them could stand Tootsie. Pierre was nervous and started squawking!

"I don't think this is going to work," said Stephanie.

"Yes it will!" said Connor. "It *has* to!"

Just then, the doorbell rang again. Matthew and his dad were leaving Ginger on their way to the mountains.

"How's everything going?" asked Matthew.

"Okay, I guess," answered Connor.

Matthew handed Connor the list of instructions. "See you in a couple of days," he said.

No sooner had Connor shut the door than Ginger bounded inside the house.

"Stop!" yelled Connor.

But it was too late—Ginger knocked over a coat rack that was standing in the hallway.

Mrs. Riley gasped. "Get that dog downstairs right now!" she said.

Connor took Ginger by the leash.

"I'll fix it, I promise!" he said as he dragged Ginger to the basement.

"Oh, what am I going to do?" said Connor.
"This is turning out to be a big mistake!"

Stephanie and Lauren looked at each other and shrugged.

"Maybe you should talk to your dad about it when he gets home," said Stephanie. "He might know what to do."

Lauren looked at the clock. "It's getting late," she said. "I've got to go home."

"Me, too," said Stephanie. "Call us if you need help."

After the girls left, Connor and Ryan stood in the basement and looked around. Sarge was chasing Tootsie all over the room. Rusty was barking, while Pierre squawked from his cage. Meanwhile, Ginger was tearing up newspapers with her teeth.

"We're in big trouble, aren't we?" said Ryan, looking up at his brother.

Just then they saw their father standing at the
top of the stairs. He had just gotten home and was
still holding his briefcase.

"Your mother and I would like to see you boys
for a minute," he said.

Connor and Ryan slowly headed upstairs to the living room. They were a little nervous as they sat down on the sofa.

Connor spoke first. "Mom, Dad, I'm really sorry about everything. Our club needed money, so I thought a pet-sitting service would be a good idea. I guess it wasn't so great after all."

"No, son, it wasn't," said Mr. Riley. "But I let you go ahead with it because I hoped you'd learn a lesson. You see, Connor, God puts parents in charge for a reason. Children don't always know what's best for themselves. They need their parents to help them along the way."

"You should have asked us before you started a pet-sitting service," said Mrs. Riley. "It would have saved you a lot of trouble."

Connor hung his head. "I really am sorry," he said.

"Me, too," added Ryan.

"We'll remember next time," said Connor. "But what can we do now?"

Mr. Riley thought for a moment. "Well," he said, "I could call some of your friends' parents. They might be willing to take some of the animals for the rest of the weekend."

"That's a great idea!" said Connor.

Mr. Riley went to the telephone and began making calls.

By the end of the evening, everything had
worked out fine. Lauren's family picked up Sarge
and Pierre, and Stephanie's parents agreed to take
Tootsie. That left Ginger, who stayed at the Rileys'
house with Connor and Ryan. The boys were very
happy their troubles were over!

The next day, the Sunny Street Kids' Club sat
under the shade tree in Connor's front yard.
Everyone was there except Matthew, who was still
in the mountains.

"Well," said Connor. "That's that! We're no longer in business as pet-sitters."

"We'll have to make new notices to let everyone in the neighborhood know," said Lauren.

"But that will use up the cash we made this weekend. *Now* how can we make money?" asked Ryan.

"I guess we'll have to do what all the other kids do," said Connor.

"What's that?" asked Stephanie.

Connor laughed. "Sell lemonade, of course!"